HAMLET
AND THE ENORMOUS CHINESE DRAGON KITE

For Deb Dailey —

Happy Reading!

With best wishes,

Brian Lies

2004

Brian Lies

Moon Mountain
PUBLISHING

North Kingstown, Rhode Island

Revised edition.
Originally published in slightly different form by Houghton Mifflin Company.

Publisher's Cataloging-in-Publication Data

Lies, Brian.
    Hamlet and the enormous Chinese dragon kite / Brian Lies.
    p. cm.
    SUMMARY: Despite the worries of his porcupine friend Quince, Hamlet
the pig tries flying an enormous red dragon kite and has an aerial adventure.
    Audience: Ages 4-8.
    ISBN 1-931659-01-X (paperback) (alk. paper)
    ISBN 1-931659-04-4 (hardcover) (alk. paper)
    [1. Kites—Fiction. 2. Pigs—Fiction. 3. Porcupines—Fiction.]
        I. Title.
PZ7.L618Ham 2002   [E]—dc20
                                              2002110413

Moon Mountain books are available in bulk and with customization for
promotional use. Contact the publisher for details.

Moon Mountain Publishing
80 Peachtree Road
North Kingstown, RI 02852
www.moonmountainpub.com

The illustrations in this book were done in watercolor on Arches hot press paper.
Title design by Alan Greco.

Printed in South Korea

10 9 8 7 6 5 4 3 2 1

For my grandmothers,
Bertha Sherwood Bonham and
Josephine Bollmann Lies

Hamlet sat on his thinking-rock at the top of the hill and watched as crisp fall leaves blew by.

Quince paced back and forth with a worried expression. But that wasn't new. Quince was always worried about *something*.

"Quince," Hamlet announced, "I've made a decision."

"Oh, no!" Quince squeaked, pacing faster. "Not again! Whenever you say that, I get a bad feeling. Remember the time you decided to go rock-climbing? I warned you not to do it. Remember when you tried painting? They still haven't fixed the town clock. And I warned you not to take swimming lessons either. But you didn't listen, and you know what happened."

"Yes, I remember," Hamlet admitted. "But this is different. This time nothing can happen. I'm going to get a kite."

"A kite?" Quince gasped. "They're dangerous! You'll get string-burn!"

Hamlet laughed and started down the path to the village.

"You're such a worrier," he told Quince, who jounced along behind him. "I'm not talking about white-water rafting, or bullfighting, or anything like that. I'm going to get a *kite*, for heaven's sake."

"People who fly kites always get string-burn. Or—or they get struck by lightning," Quince insisted, waving his paws. "You'll never catch *me* flying a kite. No, sir. It's a bad idea, Hamlet."

Hamlet's mind was on the kite he'd seen in the general store. It looked like a fierce, red Chinese dragon with big claws and a long, winding tail. He could just imagine how it would look swooping through the air at the end of a string—*his* string.

"It's a perfect day for flying kites," he declared.

When Hamlet opened the door of the general store, a bell jangled somewhere far inside. He headed straight for the kites, with Quince in tow.

"See? Isn't it *great*?" Hamlet asked, holding up the dragon kite.

Quince's jaw dropped, and his quills stood up straight. "Not that one! What if there's a knight in armor lurking in the woods, and while you're carrying the kite home, he mistakes you for a real dragon? Knights carry sharp swords, you know."

Quince held up another kite. It was tiny and squarish and the color of cold oatmeal. "How about this one? This one looks safe."

Hamlet wrinkled his nose. It was ugly. Nothing at all like the beautiful Chinese dragon kite with the fierce claws and long, winding tail. Now *that* was a kite!

Hamlet went to pay for the kite and the shopkeeper raised his eyebrows. "Kind of a big kite for such a small pig," he remarked. "Perhaps one of the smaller dragons would be better."

Quince nodded and poked Hamlet. "See? He thinks so too! Oh, there's going to be trouble! Mark my words!" He waved the tiny oatmeal-colored kite. "If you absolutely *have* to get a kite, get this one!"

But Hamlet shook his head. His mind was made up.

He gathered the kite in his arms and headed home. Quince followed, muttering in his tiny voice, "Trouble's coming! Just you wait and see. And don't come crying to me when you get carried away. Just you remember I told you so..."

Hamlet took the kite to the field near his house, where the wind was strong. He let out some string, walked back a few steps, and tugged gently. Quince started pacing.

The wind caught hold of the kite, and it soared into the sky with a *whoosh*. It danced and dodged and looped around like a real dragon. Soon the enormous kite was just a tiny red squiggle in the sky.

Hamlet felt wonderful. What a day! A swift breeze, an enormous kite, and an endless blue sky to sail it in—

Then the kite gave a strong jolt. Hamlet had come to the end of the string, and the kite tugged harder and harder. Hamlet leaned way back, but the kite pulled him up again.

"Oh, help!" Quince cried. "Fire! Flood! Disaster! Let go of the kite, Hamlet! It's too windy! Let it go!"

That was the most ridiculous thing Hamlet had ever heard. Let go of the beautiful Chinese dragon kite? *Never.*

Then the kite gave another powerful tug. Hamlet flew completely off his feet and sailed toward the trees at the far end of the field.

Quince ran along the ground beneath him, yelling, "Let go, Hamlet, jump! Jump, and I'll catch you!"

Hamlet eyed Quince's sharp quills. That didn't seem like a good idea. Besides, if he let go of the kite, he would lose it forever. So he hung on.

The kite lifted him higher and higher, and his feet scraped the tops of the trees as he passed over them. The farther up he went, the worse the idea of letting go seemed. Hamlet could still hear Quince's tiny voice shouting up at him.

"I knew it!" it squeaked. "I knew no good would come of this! Oh, help! Fire! Flood! Disaster!" But soon Quince's cries were gone, carried off by the wind.

Hamlet began to enjoy the flight, now that he was away from Quince and all of his worries. He could see the whole village from up here. "So this is what birds see," he marveled. "I'm free! It feels wonderful to fly! Quince is silly to be worried about something as fun as this!"

"Beautiful day," Hamlet said to an eagle, who was so startled to see him that she dropped the fish she was carrying home.

"A flying pig?" she cried. Then she glanced up and saw the dragon kite far above him. "Oh! I see," she nodded, with big eyes. "That dragon is kidnapping you! Well, don't you worry. We'll fix it!"

"No, I'm just flying a kite," Hamlet cried, but the eagle was already gone and didn't hear him.

Hamlet wondered what she meant by *fixing* it.

"I hope this wind dies down soon," he thought, watching the ground rush by far below. "I don't know how much longer I can hang on." He was starting to wish he had let go of the kite when Quince first suggested it.

Then the kite string made a loud noise.

Twannng!

To his horror, Hamlet saw a whole swarm of eagles high above him, attacking his beautiful kite. He yelled up at them, "Stop! It's only a kite, not a real dragon! Everything is all right! *Please* leave it alone!"

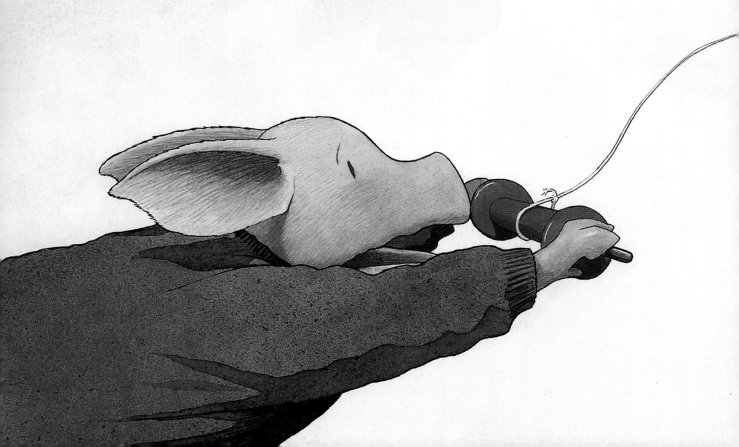

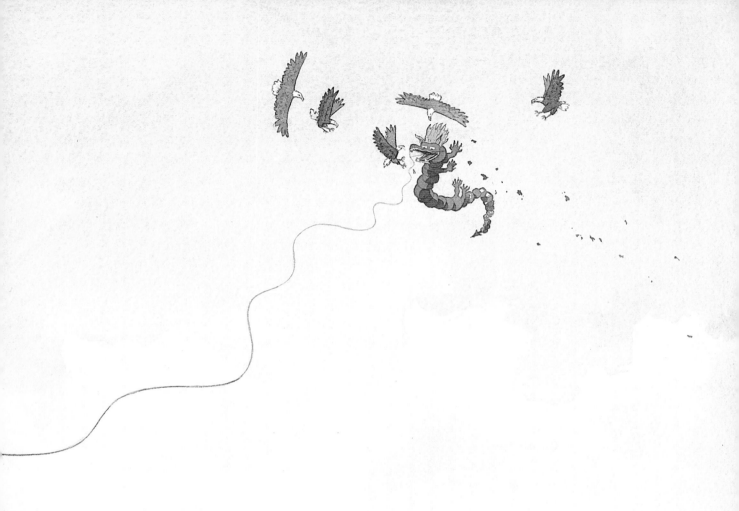

But the eagles were so far away they could barely hear him. They dived at the kite, tore it with their beaks and shredded the paper with their sharp claws—and Hamlet started to drop.

The eagles thought the dragon was trying to get away, and so they attacked it faster and harder, ripping and tearing until there wasn't anything left but broken sticks, some string, and a blizzard of red paper.

Hamlet fell faster and faster.

"Help!" he shouted. "I'm falling!"

But the eagles thought he was thanking them. They waved to him happily and swooped away home.

The ground zoomed up toward Hamlet, but he smiled at his good luck. "I'm headed straight for that pond," he grinned. "A nice, soft landing!"

The pond grew bigger and bigger as he sped toward it.

"Now I'm glad I took those swimming lessons, even though Quince said I'd get swimmer's ear or turn all wrinkly. For once I can tell *him* 'I told you so.'"

Hamlet missed the pond.

Fortunately, the kite string snarled in the branches of a gigantic tree. Hamlet hung upside down from one of the largest branches, tangled in the wreckage of the Chinese dragon kite. Once it had fierce claws and a long, winding tail. Now it looked like a pile of sticks.

"It's not funny," he told the cows who were resting in the shade of the tree. "I'm stuck! Would somebody please help me down from here?"

The cows nibbled at the kite string until Hamlet fell with a *kerthump* on the ground.

"There. That's much better," one of the cows said, as Hamlet dusted himself off.

Another cow shook her head at him and scolded, "You really shouldn't be flying in the first place, you know. You don't have the wings for it."

"I *know* that," Hamlet groaned. It was no fun to be criticized while sitting in the wreckage of his beautiful kite.

He gathered the remains of the kite under one arm, thanked the cows, and trudged homeward. It was a long, dusty walk, and it was starting to get cold.

Quince hurried out to meet Hamlet as he walked up the hill. "There you are! You have no idea how worried I've been! Are you hurt? Do you have string-burn?" Hamlet shook his head, and Quince took what was left of the kite from him. He set it gently on the rubbish heap behind the house.

"I made some hot chocolate," Quince said. "I hope you don't mind me using your kitchen, but I know how much you like hot chocolate after one of your adventures. And I even got whipped cream," he added.

Hamlet collapsed into his favorite chair and sighed as Quince handed him a steaming cup, piled high with whipped cream. *What else does a pig need*, he thought, *besides solid ground under his feet, a cup of hot chocolate, and a good friend?*
Unless...
He'd just had a brilliant idea.